Jumping Jack Rabbit

For my nephew Christopher
and my niece Caroline with love – AD

For Peter – AP

Scholastic Children's Books
Commonwealth House, 1-19 New Oxford Street
London WC1A 1NU, UK
a division of Scholastic Ltd
London ~ New York ~ Toronto ~ Sydney ~ Auckland
Mexico City ~ New Delhi ~ Hong Kong

First published in paperback in the UK by Scholastic Ltd, 2005

ISBN 0 439 95930 6

Printed in Singapore

2 4 6 8 10 9 7 5 3 1

Jumping Jack Rabbit

Alan Durant

illustrated by

Ant Parker

Jumping Jack was a rabbit who couldn't stay still.

From the moment he was born . . .

. . . he bounced

and he bobbed

and he pranced

and he hopped . . .

. . . from the cradle to the floor to the window sill.

He jumped and he jumped and he couldn't stay still.

Breakfast, lunch, dinner, he never finished a meal
Because he was up and jumping and he couldn't stay still.

'Jack Rabbit,' said his mum. 'You'll make yourself ill.'
'I can't help it,' said Jack. 'I just can't keep still.'

When he went to school with his brother Bill,

Jack jumped and he bumped right over the hill.

He bounced by the brook and the old windmill.

He hopped and he skipped and he never stayed still.

'Jack Rabbit,' said his teacher. 'You're making me dizzy.
You're up and down, up and down like a pneumatic drill!'
But Jumping Jack Rabbit just couldn't stay still.

When the children played football, Jack went in goal.

But one, two, three, four, five, six - nil!

He let in goal after goal 'cause he wouldn't stay still!

Day or night, in sunshine or rain,

Jumping Jack Rabbit bounced through the fields

And he bounced through the fields

And he bounced through the fields

Over and over and over again.

'Come inside, Jack!' called his mum. 'You'll make yourself ill.'
But Jumping Jack just couldn't stay still.

And then, one day, Jumping Jack Rabbit did get ill.

He stayed out late in the rain and he caught a chill.

He lay in bed – but even then he couldn't keep still.

He shook and he shivered and his buck teeth chattered.

His mum called the doctor. 'Come quick, my little Jack's ill!'

The doctor looked at Jack and he gave him a pill.

'He needs to rest,' he said. 'Make sure he stays still.'

Day after day Jack stayed in bed, until . . .

. . . one morning he was better and he didn't feel ill.

But he felt sad and sorry for all the worry he'd caused.
When he got up that day, something had changed -
his chill had gone, but his bounce had gone too.

Jack didn't jump or leap or prance or hop or spring or bound.
He walked quite slowly.

In class and at mealtimes he sat quite still.

'Jack's not himself,' said his mum and his brother Bill and his teacher and all the children at school.
They missed Jack's jumping.

'How can we get his bounce back?' they asked.

So they thought and they thought and they thought – and at last . . .

. . . they came up with a plan!

Next morning Jack woke up and crept out of bed.
He plodded slowly down to breakfast and there
were his mum and his brother Bill,
jumping from the table to the window sill!

On the way to school Jack's brother Bill
bounced and bounded over the hill,
past the brook and the old windmill.
He hopped and he skipped and he never stayed still.

'Jack,' said his teacher, 'this jumping's a thrill!'

She jumped up and down, up and down, like a pneumatic drill.

The children didn't care about their football skills.

They just jumped like crazy and wouldn't keep still!

'Come on, Jack!' they cried. 'You jump too!'

Jack looked and he smiled.

His back legs quivered. His front legs jiggled.

His bobtail wiggled. His long ears waggled.

And . . .

Now Jumping Jack's a rabbit who *can* stay still.

He doesn't jump in class or in the rain and make himself ill.

He doesn't jump when he should be eating his meal.

But when the time is right and he wants a thrill
Jumping Jack jumps and jumps and jumps
and he *won't* keep still!